MAX HAS SOMETHING to SAY!!!

D1301651

WRitteN AND iLLUStRAteD
BY LAURA GORDON

MAX HAS SOMETHING to SAY.
HE BARKS AND HE BARKS
EVERY DAY!

MAX HAS to SAY SOMEtHiNG iMPORtANt, it SEEMS!

OH! i think HE WANtS to GO to THE PARK!!!

CHAOS ENSUED.
tHE BARKiNG
iNCREASED!
BUt i COULDN't
REMEMBER
WHAt i DiD
WitH HiS
LEASH!!!

HE KNOCKED OVER THE LAMP!
HE'S JUMPiNG ON THE COUCH! i
MUSt FiND HiS LEASH, HE NEEDS
tO GO OUt!

iS it iN tHiS DRAWER?

DiD i HANG it iN tHE CLOSEt?

MAX iS GOiNG CRAZY AND HE JUSt CANNOt StOP it!

i LOOKED AND i LOOKED BUT i JUST COULDN'T FIND it. SHOULD i TRY MOVING THE FRIDGE? COULD THE LEASH BE BEHIND it?

BUt tHEN i HEARD

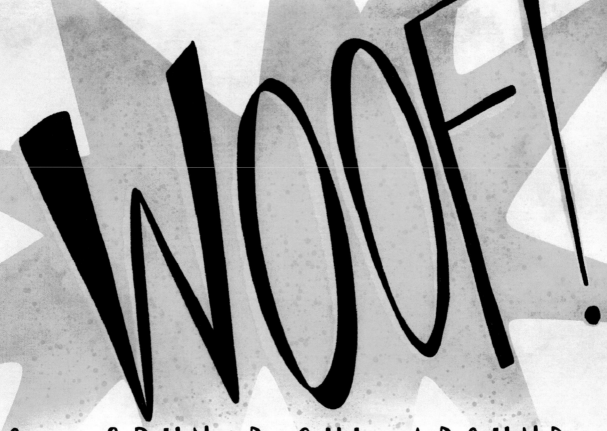

WOOF!

SO i SPUN RiGHt AROUND.
OH MAX! YOU'RE GREAt!
WHAt A MARVELOUS
HOUND!

THE LEASH WAS iN MAX'S MOUTH, HE HAD FOUND it SOMEWHERE! NOW WE CAN FiNALLY GEt SOME FRESH AiR!

HE BURST THROUGH THE DOOR AND RAN DOWN THE STREET. WE MADE it TO THE PARK! OH WHAT A TREAT!

MAX PLAYED AND HE PLAYED WITH ALL HIS DOG FRIENDS.

HE WiSHED AND HE
HOPED tHE DAY WOULDN't
END.

BUt it WAS tiME
to GO HOME, it WAS
StArtinG to GEt DARK.

POOR MAX REFUSED, HE WANTED TO STAY AT THE PARK.

BUt EVERYONE LEFt. MAX WAS tHE
ONLY DOG tHERE.
HE Still WANtED to PLAY! it JUSt
WASNt FAiR!

"COME ON!" i SAiD, LET'S GO BACK to THE HOUSE!

"YOU CAN GEt NiCE AND COZY AND CURL UP ON tHE COUCH!"

WOOF!

MAX SAID. THAT SOUNDED GOOD! HE WAS PRETTY TIRED, AND HE PROBABLY SHOULD.

ONCE WE GOt HOME, HE WENt RiGHt to SLEEP.
HE SLEPt tHROUGH tHE NiGHt WitHOUt MAKiNG A PEEP.

AND ONCE AGAIN iN THE MORNiNG, i AWOKE TO A

BARK!

"it's a new day," Max thought. let's go to the PARK!